The Girl in the Red Skirt

Lucy Cooley

As the sun rises, a thin beam of light illuminates the corn
in the sleeping meadow.
The girl in the red skirt slowly awakens.
She gently extends her arms towards the glowing ball of crimson
in the sky, and she yawns silently.
Wearily she prepares for the same journey that she makes every day.
Searching for something that she cannot find.

The girl in the red skirt hops, spins, and pirouettes
through the pastures.
She dances daily, unnoticed from dawn to dusk.
No one will hear her, she makes no noise.
No one will see her, there's no one there.
Everyone wrapped up in their own ignorance.

The girl in the red skirt sautés through the long shards of grass.
She leaps elegantly over the jagged nettles.
She twirls delicately around the daisies that thrive,
and she ascends over the precious dandelion clocks
with pure grace and elegance.

The girl in the red skirt hops, spins,
and pirouettes through the pastures.
She dances daily, unnoticed from dawn to dusk.
No one will hear her, she makes no noise.
No one will see her, there's no one there.
Everyone wrapped up in their own ignorance.

The girl in the red skirt steps stylishly around the dainty poppies.
She sways with pointed toes past the cherished weeds
that wave in rhythm with the soft breeze.
She values her surroundings, an award to be relished.
She floats towards the cattle that graze in the distance,
just beyond the closed gate.

The girl in the red skirt hops, spins,
and pirouettes through the pastures.
She dances daily, unnoticed from dawn to dusk.
No one will hear her, she makes no noise.
No one will see her, there's no one there.
Everyone wrapped up in their own ignorance.

The girl in the red skirt nudges against the horses
and she pats the heads of cows.
She vaults over gates exquisitely
and she springs over fences with ease.
She never tires and she never stops dancing.
Searching for the hope that she doesn't yet know.

The girl in the red skirt hops, spins,
and pirouettes through the pastures.
She dances daily, unnoticed from dawn to dusk.
No one will hear her, she makes no noise.
No one will see her, there's no one there.
Everyone wrapped up in their own ignorance.

The girl in the red skirt proceeds into town.
She vanishes into crowds of blank faces,
and she bumps into loaded shopping bags.
She thuds into humans barging angrily in their haste.
She scurries away without being seen.
It's always the same here.
She dislikes the city.

The girl in the red skirt hops, spins,
and pirouettes through the pastures.
She dances daily, unnoticed from dawn to dusk.
No one will hear her, she makes no noise.
No one will see her, there's no one there.
Everyone wrapped up in their own ignorance.

The girl in the red skirt returns to the grasslands.
She is surrounded by flowers that welcome her home.
Feeling suffocated by loneliness. She still believes there is hope.
Then the rain comes, pitter, patter. It taps against her bare arms
and runs down her distressed face.
The flowers wilt their heads downwards, and they cry for her.

The girl in the red skirt hops, spins,
and pirouettes through the pastures.
She dances daily, unnoticed from dawn to dusk.
No one will hear her, she makes no noise.
No one will see her, there's no one there.
Everyone wrapped up in their own ignorance.

The girl in the red skirt looks down sadly at her shoes.
They are tattered and torn, and her toes poke
sorrowfully through the tips.
Her skirt, once a bright scarlet red
that glowed in the moonlight,
now soiled, and ripped.
Her head hangs, her shoulders slump
and she falls silently to the ground.
A solo tear drops miserably down her cheek.
She doesn't want to dance. She's tired.
All hope fades away, with the light of day.
The darkness surrounds her like an unwelcome blanket.

As the sun rises once more, a thin beam of light illuminates
the corn in the sleeping meadow.
The girl in the red skirt slowly awakens.
She gently extends her arms towards the glowing ball of crimson
in the sky, and she yawns silently.
Her misty eyes glow brightly in the light of the day.
Her tears dry as the puddles evaporate.
Despair has been replaced once again, by hope.

The girl in the red skirt sees a faint rainbow in the distance.
A ballerina emerges and she dances towards her.
The girl looks exactly like her.
The girl in the red skirt sautés through the long shards of grass.
She leaps elegantly over the jagged nettles.
She twirls delicately around the daisies that thrive,
and she ascends over the precious dandelions
with pure grace and elegance.

The girl in the red skirt smiles and she holds out
a small hand for her to take hold of.
Her skirt is lustrous in the morning sunlight,
and her satin shoes gleam. She looks like she did, before.
She takes her hand, and she returns her smile.
Together they skip towards the welcoming colours of the rainbow.

The girls in the red skirts hop, spin,
and pirouette through the pastures.
They dance daily, unnoticed from dawn to dusk.
No-one will hear them, they make no noise.
No one will see them, there's no-one there.
Everyone wrapped up in their own ignorance.

Ragbag

First Edition August 2023
ISBN: 978-1-7395165-1-2 (Hardback)
ISBN: 978-1-7395165-0-5 (Paperback)

Also available on Kindle

Milton Keynes UK
Ingram Content Group UK Ltd.
UKRC031137180324
439699UK00002B/8